P9-BBT-930

Dear Alexandra

A Story of Switzerland

Written and illustrated
by Helen Güdel

Translated by Maria Moser

Soundprints
Where Children Discover...

To Ruben — H.G.

Illustrations copyright © 1999 Helen Güdel
Book copyright © 1999 Trudy Corporation, 353 Main Avenue, Norwalk, CT 06851

Soundprints is a division of Trudy Corporation, Norwalk, Connecticut.

Book design: Diane Hinze Kanzler
Editor: Judy Gitenstein

10 9 8 7 6 5 4 3 2 1
Printed in Hong Kong

Originally published as *Lieber Alex* by Atlantis Kinderbücher, a division of Verlag Pro Juventute, Zurich, Switzerland, 1991. First English-language edition (*Dear Alex*) published 1992.

Library of Congress Cataloging-in-Publication Data

Güdel, Helen.
[Lieber Alex. English]
    Dear Alexandra: a story of Switzerland / written and illustrated by Helen Güdel.
        p.   cm.
    Summary: In letters throughout the year, Alexandra's grandmother describes the routines and celebrations that make up life in her little village in the mountains of Switzerland.
    ISBN 1-56899-739-6 (hardcover) — ISBN 1-56899-740-X (pbk)
    [1. Mountain life—Switzerland—Fiction. 2. Switzerland—Fiction. 3. Grandmothers—Fiction.
4. Letters—Fiction]   I. Title.
PZ7.G935De   1999   98-51135
[Fic]—dc21   CIP
                                                                    AC

Dear Alexandra

A Story of Switzerland

Törbel, November 3

Dear Alexandra,

Can you imagine, it snowed! In the morning, when we make our way to the stable in the dark, Bruno shows me the tracks we find in the snow. He carries a flashlight. Bruno knows if it was a hare or a fox that crossed our way. When somebody has passed before us, he can tell by the footprints if that person was Josie or Felix.

Our goats are still outside, way up there on top of those cliffs where you saw them last fall. Bruno is out looking for them now. For two hours he had to work his way through the snow with a shovel before he could find Frannie and Tessie. The other three managed to escape. I'll let you know if and when he catches them.

Till then, have fun!

Dini Grossmüäter

Törbel, November 7

Dear Alexandra,

I promised to write once Bruno caught those three goats—well, he did! They were so starved they forgot to be shy and took some bread right out of his hand.

Boy, was I worried! It had turned dark already, and Bruno still had not come back. I even considered launching a rescue operation. Then, all of a sudden, I heard bells chiming in the alley. Bruno took Zilla, Babe, and Sina over to Sepp's. Sepp keeps black-neck goats too, and he has lots more room in his stable than we do.

Take care for now.

Dini Grossmüäter

Törbel, December 12

Dear Alexandra,

Today was moving day. We have finished all the hay in our stable, so we took the animals and the shovel, the pitchfork, the broom, and all the rest of our paraphernalia through the village and up into the hamlet of Hofstetten. We had a terrible time keeping the animals together. Albertine came to the rescue. She led Apollo. She knows how to handle mules very well.

Actually, before they built the road up here, most farmers did keep a mule. Fredy did all sorts of strange things along the way. He laid down in the middle of the road and rolled around in the mud. First he ran to the right, then to the left. The cows got all confused. But somehow we finally made it to the top and now all the animals are resting peacefully in the stable, with plenty of hay.

We have to move to a different stable every three to six weeks, whenever the hay is used up. We try to stay outside the village as long as we can, so that when we move back to the village, the hay will last as long as the snow is deep!

I'll write again soon.

Dini Grossmüäter

Törbel, January 6

Dear Alexandra,

I just wanted to show you what the stable here looks like. Apollo and Fredy can no longer be kept next to each other, but Fredy and Vency get along fine. The two cows, Ruby and Star, respect Apollo and fight much less now.

Unfortunately, the barn is quite a long way from here. Bruno carries hay to the animals in his big apron. He has to make at least six trips before everybody gets enough to eat. Last year's barn cat is back again, too. The hen (do you see her?) has hurt her leg. Bruno stepped on her foot with his big boots. She is allowed to stay in the stable until she gets well again.

Until next time!

Dini Grossmüäter

Törbel, March 8

Dear Alexandra,

Now the snow is gone in the village. I wish you could be with us right now. You would then see the Weisshorn shining bright in the early morning light while all the other mountains are still hiding in the mist.

The cows in the picture are Albertine's. They are coming back from the well. Albertine does not keep black Eringer cows the way we do. Her cows give more milk. But they do not know how to fight. And in Wallis, a good fight means everything in the life of a true cow!

The cats you see under Gody's window meet there every morning, waiting for him to share the leftovers from his breakfast.

Good-bye for now.

Dini Grossmüeter

13

Törbel, May 15

Dear Alexandra,

I really enjoy this great warm weather. But the whole village is complaining because everything is drying up. All conversation centers on the water situation. When the radio announces that it is raining where you live, we get jealous.

Do you remember our canals? They cover the whole mountain like a net. Now the water flows day and night there. Every farmer is allowed to use some of it to water his meadows, but only for a short time. When the shadows across the valley reach a certain point the water has to be handed over. Watering continues during the night as well, from the time you can see the first star until midnight, and from midnight until sunrise.

Bruno has raised the baby goat with a bottle. It follows him wherever he goes. Its name is Mikey. The dog, Mylord, is its best friend.

I hope you are planning to visit us soon.

Dini Grossmüäter

15

Törbel, June 29

Dear Alexandra,

Today is a most important day. We herded all cows up the alp. I always get a little bit scared on the way up. We have to be very careful not to let the cows get too close to each other. If we do, those Eringer cows immediately start fighting, and that can be dangerous. Once the cows reach the alp they each get a number. Our Ruby is number 6, and Star is number 5. At nine o'clock they are turned loose, and that's when the fighting begins. It lasts until the strongest cow wins. She is pronounced to be the queen, and she becomes famous all over the upper Wallis.

The Eringer cows look down on the other cows, those that are spotted or gray. They can't be bothered to fight with them. Once it is decided which cow is queen, the ring is opened. The cows move to the alp, the queen leading the way. The whole thing is one big celebration. Everyone joins in the fun.

Talk to you later.

Dini Grossmüäter

Törbel, July 31

Dear Alexandra,

   We could really use your help now! We are in the middle of the hay-making season. Bruno has to carry one load after the other to the barn on his back. If possible he carries it only to the path and loads it upon Apollo's sled. But once they reach the barn he has to unload and carry every bit up a tall ladder. He dumps the hay through the upper door and in winter we can easily remove it through the bottom.

   Every evening when the work is done, Albertine goes out to the field with a plastic bag and gathers all the hay that Bruno dropped!

   That's all for today. I am much too tired for writing letters!

Dini Grossmüäter

19

Törbel, September 3

Dear Alexandra,

Bruno now takes Apollo to the stables every day and empties the manure bins to make room for winter. The manure needs to be spread onto the meadows. Bruno makes up to thirty round trips a day. Many farmers have a small Caterpillar tractor for this job. But there are still people who carry the manure to the fields in a container on their backs.

Bruno is spending every day out in the fields. That's why I have the time to write to you. I wanted to show you how Apollo looks in the morning when we get him ready to carry all that manure. Bruno puts big baskets on him. He fills them with manure at the stable.

Don't be surprised to see that Sturdy, the dog in the back, is not tied down. Three times a week, Bruno takes both dogs hunting. That wears them out so much that Sturdy no longer feels like running away from home. And now I am going to give Apollo some sugar before he takes off.

See you soon.

Dini Grossmüater

21

Törbel, November 25

Dear Alexandra,

    Today is St. Martin's Fair in Visp. Bruno has been
looking forward to it for a long time now. But every time
he is somewhat disappointed, because it no longer is the
way it used to be. In the old days, cows were being traded;
now there is a parking lot where there were cows.
But occasionally there is someone around trying to sell
a few sheep or goats. People come from all over the Wallis
to this fair and every few steps Bruno runs into a friend.
He needs to buy Fredy a new harness and I am sure
he'll bring back some chestnuts. His father used to bring
chestnuts home to his children every time he went
to the fair.

I'll tell you if I was right!

Dini Grossmüäter

Törbel, November 30

Dear Alexandra,

You'll never guess what Bruno brought back from the fair—a baby goat! And it hasn't been that long since we sold Mikey, born just last spring. Now there is a crazy goat in our kitchen again! It romps with Mylord and Kittycat through the whole place. Bruno bought it for you, so you could have some fun when you come. He brought the chestnuts too, of course. With a nail he punched some holes through a pan. Now he can roast them easily.

Too bad you can't share them with us!

Dini Grossmüter

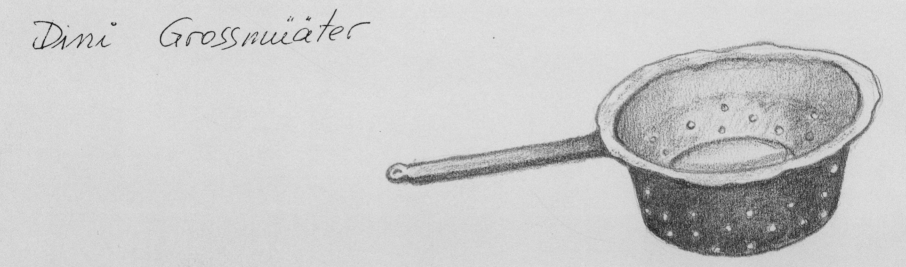

Törbel, December 15

Dear Alexandra,

Meet Ruby's daughter! She was born at two o'clock this morning and her name is Taffy. She is red, not black like her mother. Some cows stay that way, others turn black as they grow older. Kittycat joins us now every day in the stable. Just like a barn cat she too wants a bowl of fresh milk every day.

See you soon!

Dini Grossmüter

Törbel, December 20

Dear Alexandra,

   Look, your room is ready! We are all very happy that you will be spending Christmas with us. Kittycat and Mylord sense that you are coming. They have already occupied your room. Sturdy is really put out that he has to stay in his basket, but whenever we untie him, he sneaks out the door and goes hunting. You'll have to take him for long walks often.

See you Monday!

Dini Grossmüäter

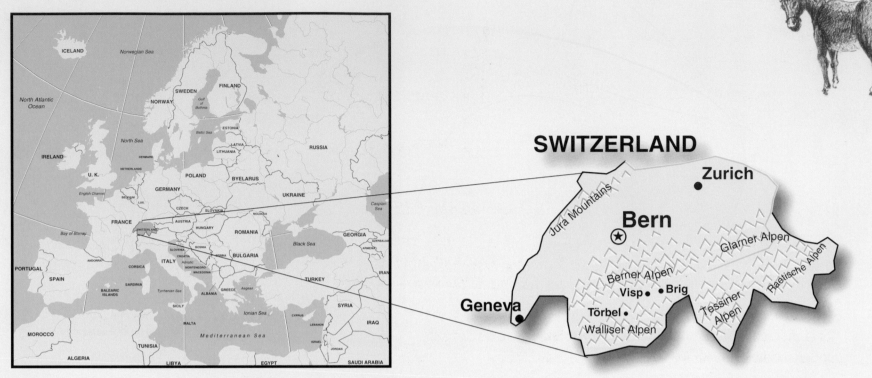

About Switzerland

Switzerland, located in central Europe, is a country of hills, valleys, evergreen forests, snow-capped mountains, waterfalls, and many lakes. It is less than sixteen thousand square miles (41,400 square kilometers) in area. The Alps mountain range covers sixty percent of the country's land area.

Switzerland is a country founded more than seven hundred years ago, in 1291, when three regions fought for independence from Austria. This is the origin of the first three cantons, or states. Today, Switzerland is officially known as the Swiss Confederation (SC) and has twenty-six cantons. It is a country of many cultures and four national languages: German, French, Italian, and Romånsh. Still, it is a tiny country, with a population of 7 million. The largest city is Zurich, with 700,000 people. The capital, Bern, where Alexandra lives, has 130,000 people.

About the village of Törbel

The story in this book takes place in the village of Törbel in the canton of Wallis. Located at an elevation of 4,500 feet, the whole area is surrounded by high mountains to the north, east, and south. To the west, there is a long valley, leading to the French part of Switzerland. Until thirty years ago, the steep slopes of the village could only be reached by foot.

Törbel is a village of only 560 inhabitants. The family names in the village today are the same ones that have been in Törbel for hundreds of years. The village is so isolated that the language, a Swiss-German dialect spoken since the fifth century, is hardly understood by people from other parts of Switzerland.

Here are some words that you might hear spoken in Törbel today:

Botsch (boch): Boy.

Chieli (kē-a'-lē): Cow.

dini Grossmüäter (dē'-nē gros'-mū-a-tar): Your grandmother.

Grossvattär (gros'-vat-ter): Grandfather.

guätän Abend (gū'-a-tan a-bend'): Good afternoon or good evening (only used for adults).

Näschi (nesh'-ē): Goat.

sali (sal'-ē): Hello (only used for children and for people you know well).

Tag wohl (tag wol): Good day (only used for adults and only until noon).

Techterli (tek'-ter-lē): Girl, daughter.

tschau (cha'-ū): Bye-bye (only used for children and for people you know well).